Just Like Heaven

PATRICK McDONNELL

LJB
1837

LITTLE, BROWN AND COMPANY
New York ∿ Boston ∿ London

Also by Patrick McDonnell:
The Gift of Nothing
Art

Little, Brown and Company • Time Warner Book Group • 1271 Avenue of the Americas, New York, NY 10020 • Visit our Web site at www.lb-kids.com

Library of Congress Cataloging-in-Publication Data: McDonnell, Patrick. Just like heaven / Patrick McDonnell.— 1st ed.   p. cm.

Summary: Having awakened from a nap to find himself surrounded by fog, Mooch the cat decides he must be in Heaven, especially when he sees that all of his loved ones are there.

ISBN-13: 978-0-316-06543-6 (hardcover)   ISBN-10: 0-316-06543-9 (hardcover)

[1. Heaven—Fiction. 2. Fog—Fiction. 3. Cats—Fiction. 4. Dogs—Fiction.] I. Title.

PZ7.M1554Jus 2006   [E]—dc22   2005035946

First Edition: October 2006   10 9 8 7 6 5 4 3 2 1   PHX   Printed in the U.S.A.   Printed on recycled paper

One day, Mooch sat under his favorite tree

and took a nap (as cats often do).

While he slept, a deep fog slowly crept in

and covered everything.

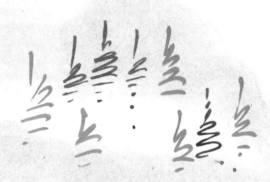

Mooch awoke.

He looked left and saw nothing.
He looked right and saw nothing.

Up, down, all around...nothing.

Mooch wondered where he was.

Heaven . . . ? he thought.

I must be in heaven!

Mooch wasn't sure what to do.
So he just sat still.

But after a while, he became curious
and set out to explore.

He felt cool dew on his little cat feet.

He smelled a sweet perfume

and heard music in the air.

Wow, thought Mooch. *What a great place.*

He walked past the playground filled with children's laughter.

He walked past the town filled with
friendly neighbors.

He paused at his own house filled with
the people he loved.

So this is heaven, thought Mooch.

Then Mooch came upon a big dog chained in a yard.

The big dog growled (as unloved dogs often do)

and let out a BIG BARK.

In the past, Mooch would have gone all fuzzy with fear and run away.

But here and now, Mooch wondered,
What would you do in heaven?

So he opened his arms and said...

"Hug Time!"

And they did.

Wow, thought Mooch. *What a great place.*

Mooch continued exploring

until he ended back at his favorite tree

and took another nap (as cats often do).

Slowly the fog lifted

and the sun shone through.

Mooch awoke

to find his best friend, Earl, sleeping
under their favorite tree.

Wow, thought Mooch. *What a great place.*

Just like heaven.